This book belongs to

- -

For Jack

Paperback edition first published in 2016
First published in hardback Great Britain in 2015 by
words & pictures, an imprint of Quarto Publishing Plc,
The Old Brewery, 6 Blundell Street, London N7 9BH

British Library Cataloguing in Publication Data available on request

ISBN 978 1 78493 998 4

1 3 5 7 9 8 6 4 2

Printed in China

Mr Hare's BIG Secret

Hannah Dale

words & pictures

In the wild, wild wood there stood a big, tall tree.
And under that tree lived a very hungry hare.

Now, as everyone knows, hares are very clever.
And Mr Hare was especially clever, because
he knew a big, fat, juicy secret.

Miss Mouse scurried by, snuffling and sniffling among the leaves.

"Hello there, Miss Mouse," said Mr Hare. "Would you like to know my secret?"

Now, as everyone knows, mice are very curious. And Miss Mouse was especially curious.

"Ooh, yes, please, Mr Hare, I love secrets!"

"Well, if you *really* want to know my secret,
then you must dance with me first,
right here underneath this tree."

In the wild, wild wood
there stood a big, tall tree.
And under that tree, Mr Hare hopped
and Miss Mouse jiggled.

When Mr Fox came by,
he stopped to stare.
What a sight!
A jiggling mouse and a hopping hare!

"Yoohoo, Mr Fox!" called Miss Mouse.
"Do you want to know Mr Hare's secret?"
    Now, as everyone knows, foxes love secrets.
And Mr Fox especially loved secrets.
    "Ooh, yes, please, Mr Hare, I love secrets!"

"Well, if you *really* want to know my secret,
then you must dance with us first,
right here underneath this tree."

In the wild, wild wood there stood a big, tall tree.
And under that tree, Mr Hare hopped,
Miss Mouse jiggled and Mr Fox trotted.

When busy Mrs Duck came by, she stopped to stare.
What a sight!
A trotting fox, a jiggling mouse and a hopping hare!

"Oh, busy Mrs Duck!" cried Mr Fox.
"Do you want to know Mr Hare's secret?"
Now, as everyone knows, ducks are very forgetful.
And Mrs Duck was especially forgetful.
She had completely forgotten why she was so busy!
"Ooh, yes, please, Mr Hare, I love secrets!"

"Well, if you *really* want to know my secret,
then you must dance with us first,
right here underneath this tree."

In the wild, wild wood there stood a big, tall tree.
And under that tree, Mr Hare hopped,
Miss Mouse jiggled, Mr Fox trotted and
Mrs Duck wiggled.

When grumpy Mr Frog leaped by,
he stopped to stare.
What a sight!
A wiggling duck, a trotting fox,
a jiggling mouse and a hopping hare!

"Grumpy Mr Frog!" called busy Mrs Duck.
"Do you want to know Mr Hare's secret?"
  Now as everyone knows, frogs can be very cross.
  And grumpy Mr Frog was especially cross
because Mr Hare knew a secret that he didn't.

"Hmph!" said grumpy Mr Frog.
"Well, yes, I really would like to know the secret."
"Well, if you *really* want to know my secret,
then you must dance with us first,
right here underneath this tree."

In the wild, wild wood
there stood a big, tall tree.
And under that tree, Mr Hare hopped,
Miss Mouse jiggled, Mr Fox trotted,
Mrs Duck wiggled and Mr Frog leaped.

When Mr Owl flew by, he stopped to stare.
What a sight! A leaping frog,
a wiggling duck, a trotting fox,
a jiggling mouse and a hopping hare!

Now, as everyone knows, owls are very wise.
And Mr Owl was especially wise.
So, soon, Mr Owl had guessed Mr Hare's secret,
because all that hopping, jiggling, trotting . . .

. . . wiggling and leaping had made his branch shiver and shake.

Then, with a plop and a plip . . .

. . . the ground under the big, tall tree
was covered in
big,
fat,
juicy cherries.

As the moon rose over the wild, wild wood,
a very tired Mr Hare stretched out
with a big, round and very full tummy . . .

...and he wasn't hungry any more.